C

HIT

Please renew or return items by the date
shown on your receipt

www.hertfordshire.gov.uk/libraries

Renewals and enquiries: 0300 123 4049

Textphone for hearing or 0300 123 4041
speech impaired users:

L32 11.16

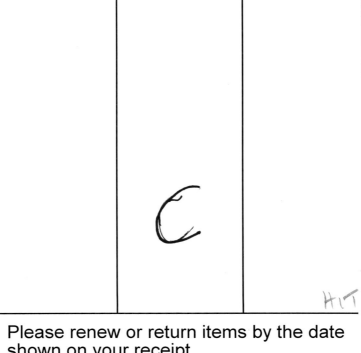

D1362942

First published 2007 by Walker Books Ltd
87 Vauxhall Walk, London SE11 5HJ

This edition published 2017

2 4 6 8 10 9 7 5 3 1

This book has been typeset in Windsor

Printed in China

British Library Cataloguing in Publication Data:
a catalogue record for this book is available
from the British Library

ISBN 978-1-4063-7331-8

www.walker.co.uk

MIX
Paper from
responsible sources
FSC® C101537
FSC
www.fsc.org

Penguin

Polly Dunbar

WALKER BOOKS
AND SUBSIDIARIES

LONDON · BOSTON · SYDNEY · AUCKLAND

Ben ripped open his present.

Inside was a penguin.

"Hello, Penguin!" said Ben.

"What shall we play?" said Ben.

Penguin said nothing.

"Can't you talk?" said Ben.

Penguin said nothing.

Ben tickled Penguin.

Penguin didn't laugh.

Ben pulled his funniest face
for Penguin.

Penguin didn't laugh.

Ben put on a happy hat

and sang a silly song

and did a dizzy dance.

Penguin said nothing.

"Will you talk to me if I stand on
my head?" said Ben.

Penguin didn't say a word.

So Ben prodded Penguin

and blew a raspberry at Penguin.

Penguin said nothing.

Ben made fun of Penguin

and imitated Penguin.

Penguin said nothing.

Ben ignored Penguin.

Penguin ignored Ben.

So Ben fired Penguin into outer space ...

Penguin came back to Earth without a word.

Ben tried to feed Penguin
to a passing lion.

Penguin said nothing.

Lion didn't want to eat Penguin.

Ben got upset.

Penguin said nothing.

Lion ate Ben

for being too noisy.

Penguin bit Lion
very hard
on the nose.

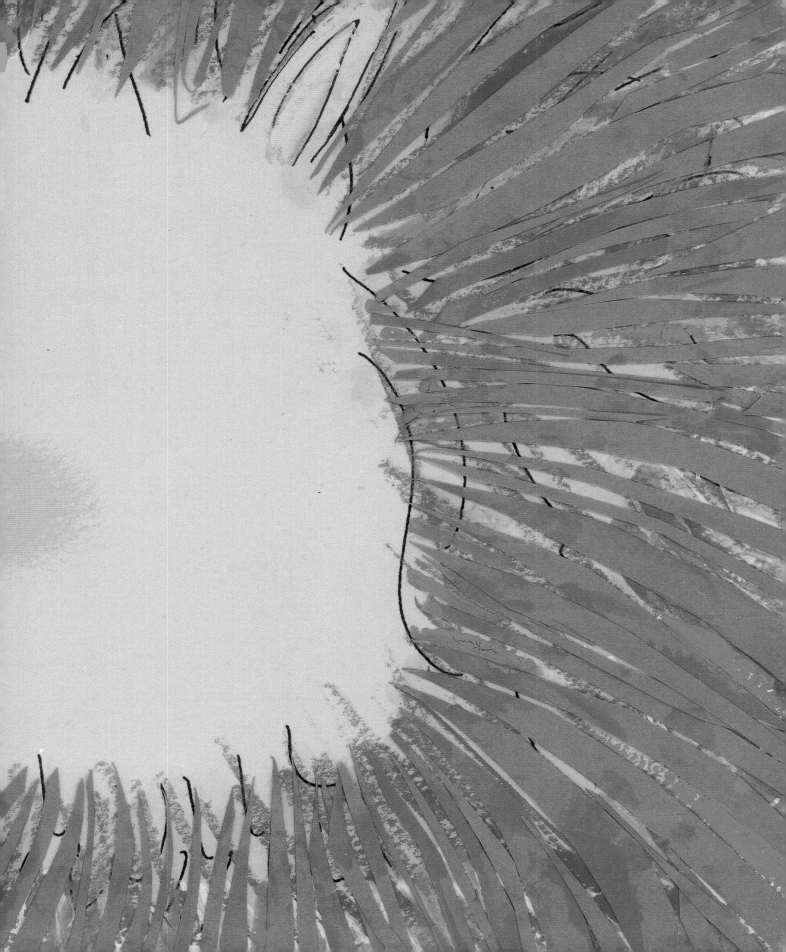

 said Lion.

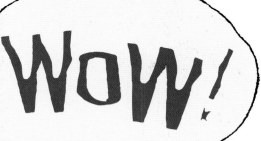 said Ben.

And Penguin said ...

everything!

Polly Dunbar
is the author-illustrator of *Arthur's Dream Boat* and *Dog Blue*. She is also the illustrator of *Shoe Baby* and *Pat-a-Cake Baby*, both written by her mother, Joyce Dunbar, and *My Dad's a Birdman*, written by David Almond. Her collection of titles beginning with *Hello Tilly* was made into an animation series, *Tilly and Friends*, as seen on CBeebies. She is the co-founder of Long Nose Puppets, a children's theatre company. Polly lives in Beccles, Suffolk.